Alma Flor Ada • F. Isabel Campoy

SINGING HORSE

ILLUSTRATORS

Enrique Martínez
Felipe Dávalos
Isaac Hernández
Fabricio Vanden Broeck
Claudia Legnazzi
Gloria Calderas
Carmen Cardemil

ALFAGUARA
YOUNG READERS
SANTILLANA

Originally published in Spanish as *Mambrú*

Art Director: Felipe Dávalos
Design: Petra Ediciones
Editor: Norman Duarte

Cover: Enrique Martínez

Santillana USA Publishing Company, Inc.
2105 NW 86th Avenue
Miami, FL 33122

Poetry C: *Singing Horse*

ISBN: 1-58105-579-X

Printed in Colombia
Grupo OP S.A.

ILLUSTRATORS

GLORIA CALDERAS: pp. 24-27
CARMEN CARDEMIL: pp. 28-32
FELIPE DÁVALOS: p. 8
ISAAC HERNÁNDEZ: pp. 10-13
CLAUDIA LEGNAZZI: pp. 20-23
ENRIQUE MARTÍNEZ: pp. 6, 7, 9
FABRICIO VANDEN BROECK: pp. 14-19

ACKNOWLEDGEMENTS

The authors gratefully acknowledge the editorial assistance of Susan Baird Kanaan
and Rosa Zubizarreta.

ROSA ZUBIZARRETA for the English translation of the following poems:
Alma Flor Ada, "Seashell," p.8; F. Isabel Campoy, "To José Antonio Dávila," p.11;
Alicia Barreto de Corro, "Surprise," p.16; José Antonio Dávila, "What Is Most
Valuable," p. 12.

Translations and/or adaptations are based on the following works.
JOSÉ ANTONIO DÁVILA: "Lo que más vale," "Lección," and "La cebolla" from
La poesía del niño compiled by Isabel Freire de Matos. Copyright ©1993, Instituto
de Cultura Puertorriqueña. Permission to use these works is pending.
ALICIA BARRETO DE CORRO: "Sorpresa," "¡Cómo trabajas!," "Los peces," and
"¿Caminan?" from *Viaje de la hormiga*. Copyright © Gráficas Los Morros. Reprinted
by permission of the author.
JUAN BAUTISTA GROSSO: "Amor infantil" and "Mi Hermosa casa" from
Reír cantando. Copyright ©1954, Hachette. "Los pescadores" from
La poesía y el niño compiled by Isabel Freire de Matos. Copyright ©1993, Instituto
de Cultura Puertorriqueña. Permission to use these works is pending.
FRANCISCO JOSÉ GABILONDO SOLER: "La patita" and "El chorrito" from *Cancionero
mexicano* compiled by Luisa Valdivia. Copyright ©1988 Consejo Nacional de
Fomento Educativo. Reprinted by permission of María Teresa Gallegos Venegas.
ÁNGELA FIGUERA AYMERICH: "Jugando" and "El pirata piratón" from *Cuentos tontos
para niños* by Ángela Figuera Aymerich. Copyright ©1985, Editorial Trillas.
Reprinted by permission of Editorial Trillas.
"El río y los pájaros" from *Canciones para todo el año* by Angela Figuera Aymerich.
Copyright ©1984, Editorial Trillas. Permission to use this work is pending.

To Alma and Mireya Lafuente, sisters,
sources of inspiration
for the courage to begin anew.

Contents

Latinos

Puerto Rico

Venezuela

Latinos

From Everywhere

F. Isabel Campoy

We live in the United States.
We come from North America,
Central and South America.
We were born on islands, in deserts,
in Chicago, and in New York.
We are of every race,
and every color,
yet our grandmothers spoke Spanish.
We are bilingual,
with twice as much to offer.

Alma Flor Ada

Alma Flor Ada is a Cuban author
who has written many, many books for children.
Her name might be right out of a fairy tale.
She shares the name Alma with her mother
and the name Flor with her sister.
Ada is her father's last name.

She has four children and eight grandchildren.
Alma Flor is a professor at the University of San Francisco.

She loves water, both for drinking
and for swimming.

To Alma Flor Ada

F. Isabel Campoy

Poetry visits you,
as good friends do,
at any time,
without notice.
And your laughter
hangs from the trees
around your house,
encouraging passers-by
to live more fully.

Your voice is hope's embrace;
your steps, the way to peace.

Seashell

Alma Flor Ada

Seashell, seashell,
on the shore,
beneath the sun.

Under the sun,
tossed by the sea,
seashell you will always be.

You'll always be
mother of pearl
on the shore,
beneath the sun.

Beneath the sun,
beneath the moon,
seashell made of ocean
  foam.

Longing

Alma Flor Ada

The breeze in the coconut tree
wants to go and swim in the sea.
But the coconut tree won't say good-by;
he wants the breeze to stay nearby.
The breeze sighs and pleads with emotion;
she wants to go and play in the ocean.
To keep her happy and entranced,
the coconut tree invites her to dance.

Sleep falls upon the coconut tree
(he is not the dancer he used to be),
while the breeze silently slips away
to play with the waves that
        toss in the bay.
She dresses the waves up in
        lacey froth
back and forth and forth
        and back.
The moon is as happy as
        happy can be
watching the breeze play with
        the sea.

Puerto Rico

The Voice of Puerto Rico

F. Isabel Campoy

The voice of Puerto Rico
is bright.
We can hear it
day and night.

The voice of Puerto Rico
is clear,
and you can hear it
everywhere.

The voice of Puerto Rico
is bright, clear, and strong,
like the little tree frog's song.

José Antonio Dávila

This Puerto Rican poet
wrote a beautiful book of poems
called *Almacén de Baratijas* (Warehouse of Trinkets).
He dedicated it to his niece, who was an inspiration for his writing.
Some of his poems are based on legendary figures, such as the
pirate Cofresí.

José Antonio Dávila was the son of another
great poet, Virgilio Dávila, who wrote well-loved poems
about life in rural Puerto Rico.

To José Antonio Dávila

F. Isabel Campoy

Pirate of the fields
who guards
a million stars
in your rich coffers,
allow me to sit beneath
the sky of your imagination
while you tell me a story,
just you and I.

What Is Most Valuable

José Antonio Dávila

Nobody can live
without sun, without wind,
without water.
While these things are the most valuable things of all,
they don't cost anything.
God gives them to us as a gift.

Lesson

José Antonio Dávila

I would like to learn,
if anyone knows,
how to fashion with my hands
the petals of a rose.

Lady Onion

José Antonio Dávila

Lady Onion, I am told,
is so afraid to catch a cold
that she puts on a warm white shawl,
and then another,
and another…

And just like the tale
about the rooster,
you know my story
doesn't end here.

13

Venezuela

Blue Country

Alma Flor Ada
F. Isabel Campoy

Blue country,
as the waters of your seas.

Green country,
as the heart of your forests.

Beautiful country,
with birds of a thousand hues.

Alicia Barreto de Corro

She looks at the world
with playful and wondering eyes,
and then wants to tell us all about it.
Her sons Leoncio and Leonardo
were always her best readers.
They also illustrated her first book of poems,
Viaje de la hormiga (*The Ant's Journey*).
Another beautiful book of hers is
Dice la negra Hipólita (*Old Hipólita Says*).

To Alicia Barreto de Corro

F. Isabel Campoy

Alicia,
inventor of continents
where ants work,
and live and play.

Alicia,
take us to the constellation
where your imagination
weaves laughter and sleight-of-hand.

And please send us your address
in Wonderland.

Surprise

Alicia Barreto de Corro

Look, look, a leaf is walking.
No, no,
an ant is walking.

16

How Hard You Work

Alicia Barreto de Corro

Little ant,
you work all night,
you work the whole day long.
How did you ever
come to be so strong?

17

Fish

Alicia Barreto de Corro

The little fish
do not shiver;
they snuggle beneath the covers
of the waters of the river.

Do They Run?

Alicia Barreto de Corro

How do clouds
race by
without any feet?

Argentina

Far, Far to the South

Alma Flor Ada

Far, far to the south,
by the frozen land of Antarctica,
your great plains spread wide.

In the wide-open pampas,
the majestic ombú offers its shade,
while off in the distance,
a tireless emu races
towards the setting sun.

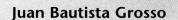

Juan Bautista Grosso

To him every subject seemed worthwhile.
He wrote short, sweet little poems
about all kinds of things.
Many of his verses praise his country, Argentina.
He published his poems in the book *Reír cantando*
(*Laughing and Singing*).

To Juan Bautista Grosso

Alma Flor Ada

In your poems,
a rainbow shines,
butterflies flutter about,
crickets leap,
and teddy bears
wake up to play
while a frolicking gnome dances.

A Child's Love

Juan Bautista Grosso

My grandpa is a dream,
my grandma is a song,
my aunts and uncles and cousins
are pieces of my love.

My Beautiful House

Juan Bautista Grosso

On a narrow green road,
I have a beautiful home
Where goldfinches sing,
and butterflies roam.

Fishermen

Juan Bautista Grosso

At dawn,
the fishermen
put out to sea
in their little boats.
They take their nets
and their songs,
these brave men
of the sea.

When night falls,
they return to the harbor
loaded down
with the day's catch.
Black corvina,
pike and sole,
oysters and hake,
and much, much more.

When night falls
and kisses the homes
of the simple
sea folks,
the breeze sings
their boats to sleep
with a lullaby
of the sea.

LA REINA DEL PLATA

23

Mexico

Today in the Future

Alma Flor Ada

Mexico, green.
Mexico, dry.
Mexico, sea.
Mexico, desert.
Mexico, joyful with its piñatas.
Mexico, sentimental with its guitars.

Mexico, indigenous,
    Spanish and mestizo.
Mexico, with roots
in the ancient past.
Mexico, creating
    the present
    and the future.

24

Francisco José Gabilondo Soler

Francisco José Gabilondo Soler is known
to children as *el Grillito Cri Cri* (*Cree Cree the Cricket*).
For many years he had a children's radio program
in Mexico that was heard all over Latin America.
Children loved his voice, his poems, his stories,
and his songs. Many of us as children learned to
write poetry inspired by his work.
How wonderful that children today are still able
to listen to him on the recordings he left for us!

To Francisco José Gabilondo Soler

Alma Flor Ada

The singing cricket is chirping
over the waves of the radio
while we are carried away
on the colorful wings of your song.

The colorful wings of your song
are both poetry and story.
You offer life lessons to all
as you chirp in all your glory.

Cree Cree, the singing cricket,
you filled my childhood with joy.
I send you a hug and a kiss
on the radio-waves of love

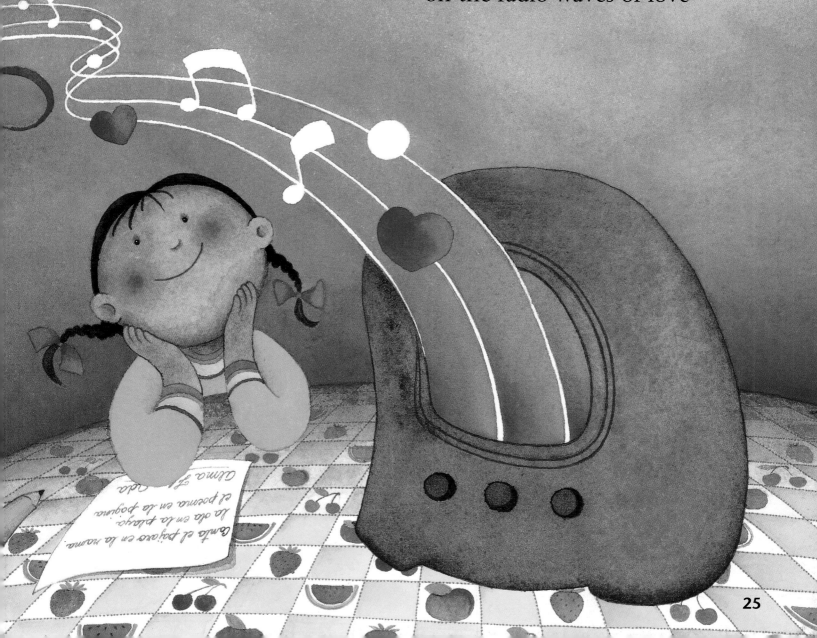

Mama Duck

Francisco José Gabilondo Soler

Mama Duck
with her basket and her shawl
sets off to market
to buy what she needs,
rocking to and fro,
like a ship in the high seas.

Mama Duck
scurries on, digging in her purse
for some coins to buy food.
Her ducklings back at home,
are hungry, and she knows
when she returns they will ask,
"What did you bring me, Mama?
What did you bring me, quack, quack?"

Fountain

Francisco José Gabilondo Soler

The cloud sends a drop of rain
to the flower down below.
The drop turns to fog again
as the sun's rays glow.

The drop climbs back up to the sky,
up to the cloud, but not for long.
It comes down again, and up again,
all to the rhythms of this little song.

In the middle of the fountain
was a little spout of water.
Sometimes it rose high,
sometimes it did not.
The unhappy little water spout
was feeling very hot.

Spain

In a Wooden Ship

F. Isabel Campoy

Spain is a far away country
that didn't want any borders
and set out to sea one day
in a wooden ship that was made to order.

The language I speak came on that boat
along with my grandfather,
his hands full of hope.

Ángela Figuera Aymerich

This writer, born in Spain, spent many years in Mexico.
She wrote several novels for adult readers and, for her
grandchildren, two books you will enjoy:
Canciones para todo el año (*Songs for All Year Long*)
and *Cuentos tontos para niños listos* (*Silly Tales for Smart Children*).

To Ángela Figuera Aymerich

F. Isabel Campoy

In your birthplace, the city of Bilbao,
both Basque and Spanish are spoken,
and children go for walks
between the river and the sea.

Today among the factories
an amazing monster rises up,
its curved walls a bright lure
to all who walk by.
This Guggenheim monster,
this lovely museum of art,
I offer to you, who have always
     been a master
at seeing beauty with your heart.

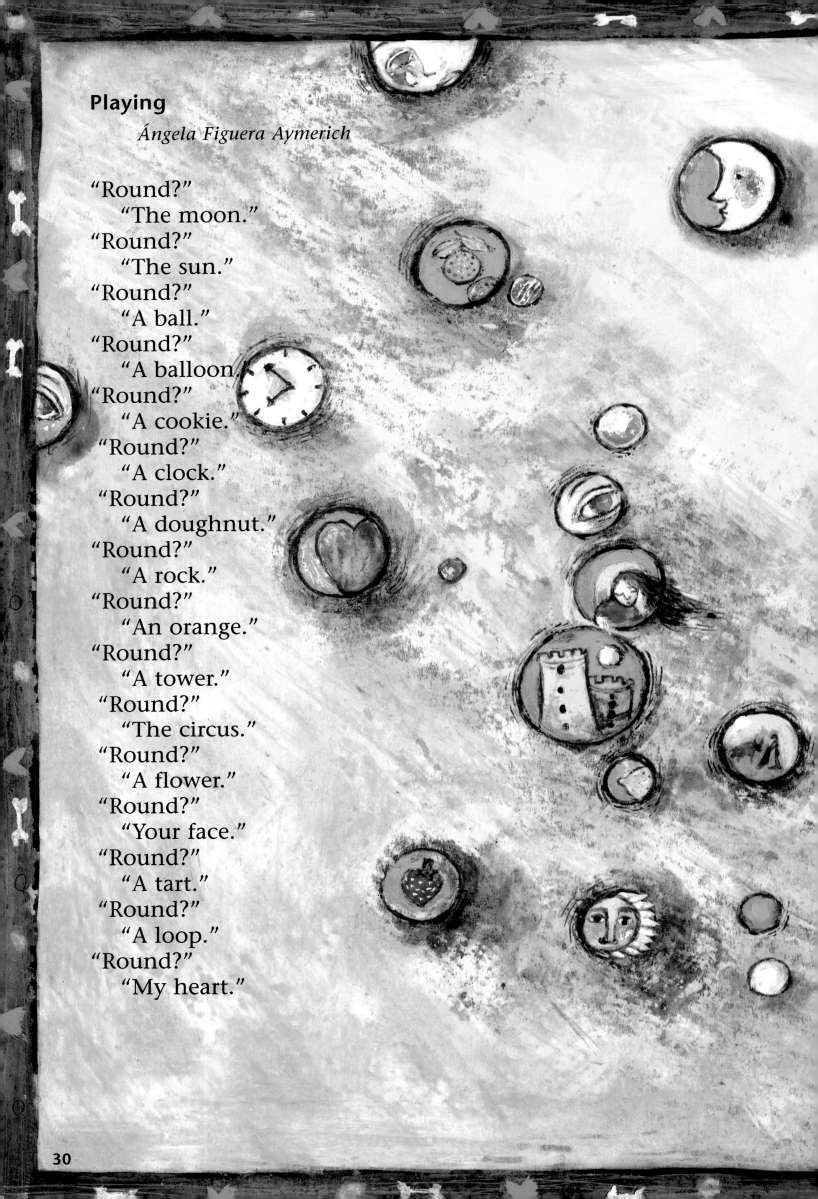

Playing

Ángela Figuera Aymerich

"Round?"
  "The moon."
"Round?"
  "The sun."
"Round?"
  "A ball."
"Round?"
  "A balloon."
"Round?"
  "A cookie."
"Round?"
  "A clock."
"Round?"
  "A doughnut."
"Round?"
  "A rock."
"Round?"
  "An orange."
"Round?"
  "A tower."
"Round?"
  "The circus."
"Round?"
  "A flower."
"Round?"
  "Your face."
"Round?"
  "A tart."
"Round?"
  "A loop."
"Round?"
  "My heart."

The Very Piratical Pirate
Ángela Figuera Aymerich

In the whole wide world
there was never
an uglier pirate, no, not ever.
He was missing one eye
and at least half an ear.
He'd lost seven teeth
it would appear.
So bad was this pirate
and oh, so very mean,
he had (guess what!)
four wooden legs
instead of one.

The River and the Birds

Ángela Figuera Aymerich

The river had fish,
gold and silver fish in his shallow waters.
The river had fish,
but what he wanted were birds.

His watery green eyes
kept looking up to the skies.

How he envied the wind,
pierced by their flight,
tickled by their beaks,
thrilled by their songs.

The river had fish,
but what he wanted were birds.